Wallace & Gromit

A MATTER OF LOAF AND DEATH

Novelization

EGMONT
We bring stories to life

First published in Great Britain 2008
by Egmont UK Limited
239 Kensington High Street, London W8 6SA

© and ™ Aardman Animations Ltd. 2008. All rights reserved.
Wallace and Gromit © and ™ Aardman Animations Limited.
Based on characters created by Nick Park.

ISBN 978 1 4052 4446 6
1 3 5 7 9 10 8 6 4 2

Printed in Italy

No part of this publication may be reproduced, stored in a retrieval system, or transmitted, in any form or by any means, electronic, mechanical, photocopying, recording or otherwise without the prior permission of the publisher and copyright owner.

Wallace & Gromit

A MATTER OF LOAF AND DEATH

Novelization

Adapted from the screenplay by Penny Worms

Screenplay by Nick Park and Bob Baker

Contents

Preamble: Baker Found Dead...................................1

Chapter 1: Top Bun: Dough-to-Door Delivery.........3

Chapter 2: A Good Day's Work...............................11

Chapter 3: Crocs Away!...17

Chapter 4: Until We Meet Again............................24

Chapter 5: A Woman's Touch..................................28

Chapter 6: Gromit Discovers a Terrible Secret.......33

Chapter 7: And it Gets Worse!................................43

Chapter 8: You Can't Be Too Careful.....................47

Chapter 9: Fluffles to the Rescue............................55

Chapter 10: Roll on Tea-Time!................62

Chapter 11: Bombs Away!......................68

Chapter 12: Great Minds Think Alike.........79

Chapter 13: A Cup of Tea Cures All..........84

Preamble:

Baker Found Dead

Baker Bob was a happy baker. Always up before the lark and never one to complain. He was particularly happy on the day he died, and not just because business was booming. Baker Bob had just won the 'Better Baker' runner-up prize for his melt-in-the-mouth shortbread. *And* he was in love again. Life was good. That was why he was singing that fateful morning as he kneaded his dough. He didn't hear the killer slip into the bakery, and it took him a second to realise that his hat had been lifted from his head. When he span around, the rolling-pin-wielding murderer dealt the fatal blow. Baker Bob was left face-down in his dough – a waste of a good life, as well as a waste of good bread.

R.I.P. Baker Bob

Chapter 1

Top Bun: Dough-to-Door Delivery

Gromit was in the kitchen reading the *The Daily Grind*. The headlines read: *"Baker Bob Murdered! 12th Baker Found Dead this Year. Cereal Killer Strikes Again."*

It made grim reading, especially to all those in the bread business like Wallace and Gromit. Their new bakery was up-and-running and they had loyal customers all over town. It had been quite a challenge turning their semi-detached house into a working windmill, but with a little of Wallace's inventiveness and a lot of Gromit's hard work, they had managed it.

Downstairs, they had converted the kitchen into an industrial-scale bakery, with mixing machines and bakery ovens. The windmill sails on the front of the house were now working perfectly, providing enough wind power to turn the huge millstone installed in Wallace's bedroom. The sails had a dual purpose too, as rotating advertising boards emblazoned with: *"Top Bun, Wallace and Gromit's Traditional Bakery"*.

At five a.m. sharp, Wallace's alarm clock sprang to life. It was time for him to get up. The Top Bun customers expected freshly baked bread first thing in the morning, and it was Wallace and Gromit's job to deliver. But the alarm clock was having no effect. Wallace had stuffed his ears full of cotton wool so he could get to sleep. It wasn't easy dropping off with your bed next to a working millstone, grinding wheat into flour day and night.

Gromit, who had been up for hours baking the bread, decided to switch to a more ingenious method of waking Wallace up. He filled a balloon with water and hooked it on to a windmill sail as it passed the kitchen window. As the windmill turned, the balloon was carried up, up, up to the top, where it dropped from the sail and fell through a skylight in the roof. It was a direct hit. The balloon burst on to Wallace's face and the water woke him from a lovely cheesy dream.

"Oh . . . Uhhh!" he spluttered. "I was just getting up, lad!"

Downstairs, Gromit was now manoeuvring a

forklift truck to remove a large batch of loaves from the ovens. On hearing Wallace's call, he put the forklift into reverse so he could hit the 'Get-U-Up' lever on the kitchen wall. Then Gromit went back to the ovens where his loaves were now crusted to perfection.

The activation of the Get-U-Up system set cogs and pulleys in motion. In an instant, a hydraulic system under Wallace's bed started to tip up the headboard end. Wallace disappeared under the sheets and shot out from the foot of the bed. With precision timing, a metal chute from the mill grinder swung round to receive him and Wallace slid down the chute along with the batches of newly ground flour.

"With you in a jiffy . . ." he called to Gromit as he fell. "Tally ho!"

It was a fast and thrilling helter-skelter of a ride

as he whizzed passed all the machinery, cogs and wheels that drove the mill. It was like travelling down a stainless steel bobsleigh run without the bobsleigh – just his pyjamas preventing any serious skin burn.

At the bottom of the chute was a gigantic mixing bowl, with electric whisks whizzing around, mixing the falling flour into the dough mixture.

"Oh no!" Wallace cried as he saw where he was heading. He'd forgotten to reset the machine last night from MIXING to BAGGING. He was going be churned up and made into burger baps! But as always Gromit was in control. At the last second, he pushed the chute gently round and Wallace continued on his freefall down another channel, heading towards the sack room. He catapulted off the end and landed neatly in his trousers, which were lined up ready for him on the flour-sack turnstile. Wallace was then tipped up, and landed head first into the baker's hat waiting for him on a conveyor belt of cottage loaves heading for the loading bay. The final stage of the Get-U-Up system – a large robotic hand – pushed Wallace off the conveyor belt and into the waiting Top Bun van. Wallace made a mental note to reset the system before he went to bed. He didn't want *that* kind of scare again.

Meanwhile, Gromit had loaded the last of the freshly baked loaves and cakes into the back of the van and was now filling up the tank with diesel from the fuel pump. Wallace's mug appeared out of the van window. Gromit switched the pump from Diesel to Tea and filled up the mug. With both van and Wallace fully fuelled, Gromit jumped into the van and activated the garage door. It lifted up like a giant bread bin and the Top Bun van sped out to start its rounds.

"Ah, lovely cuppa, Gromit," Wallace said, slurping his tea as Gromit drove. "But, um . . . a slightly diesel-y aftertaste, perhaps? How's that breakfast coming along?"

Gromit pressed the button on the cassette player in the dashboard and out popped a slice of toast.

"Hey, heh! Well done lad," said Wallace, patting Gromit on the head and crushing his baker's hat. "Mmm . . ." said Wallace, looking at the burnt toast. "It's very well done! But thanks chuck!"

Gromit picked up the newspaper and showed Wallace the headlines.

"Oh dear!" said Wallace. "Another baker. Battered! And with his own rolling pin. Would you credit it?" He finished off his toast. "Still, looking on the bright side . . ."

Gromit wrinkled his brow. Just what was the bright side of yet another baker being killed?

". . . I suppose it means more business for us, eh Gromit?" Wallace never was one to let a grisly murder affect a bright and cheery morning. "Way-hey! We're on a roll, lad!"

Chapter 2

A Good Day's Work

Wallace and Gromit's Top Bun delivery round was a slick operation. First they had to supply all the businesses across town, from Pat O'Cake's Patisserie on the east side of town to Bert's Butty Bar on the west. After visiting the sandwich shops and other big customers, they went around the neighbourhoods to deliver the householders' daily bread, launching loaves like newspapers, out of the van window through people's letterboxes and into their mailboxes.

"Good day's work, lad," Wallace said cheerfully, as he was about to deliver the last loaf. "We're bang on . . ." Wallace's voice trailed off. He had suddenly seen a vision on the horizon. It was a lady on a bike, lit up by the sun, her all-white dress billowing in the wind. She was freewheeling towards them, with a little white poodle in her basket. Wallace was so mesmerized that angels started singing in his head. He couldn't even avert his gaze to lob the last loaf out of the window towards the mailbox of number forty-seven, which was unlucky for a little old woman who was walking along the pavement outside. She was knocked sideways over a fence by the flying bread. Wallace didn't even notice.

As she passed, the lady on the bike rang her bell and waved. Wallace couldn't believe it.

"Gromit! Did you see who that was?" he asked excitedly. The angels in Wallace's head were singing: *"Light as a feather . . . You're the Bake-O-Lite girl . . ."* a jingle from an old TV advert. It had been one of the first colour adverts on TV and its impact on the nation was huge.

From the first time he had seen her, Wallace had been captivated by the Bake-O-Lite girl. She floated on to the screen suspended from a hot-air balloon on a swing. As she glided through the sunlit sky, she looked a vision of feminine loveliness. 'Get slimmer with Bake-O-Lite bread' was the slogan, and it was the most successful advertising campaign of the day.

Within weeks, every woman was eating it, hoping to look like the Bake-O-Lite girl. And there was no doubt in Wallace's mind; it was that very same Bake-O-Lite girl who had just cycled passed them, *in real life!* She was older and rounder, but to Wallace she was still a vision of loveliness.

Wallace was shaken from his daydream by a scream. Oh no! The Bake-O-Lite girl was in trouble!

With a sharp hand-brake turn, Wallace was off in pursuit of the damsel in distress.

As they got closer, they could see the lady pulling on the brakes but it was having no effect. The bike was heading downhill and gaining speed. Even the poodle looked scared.

"Here Gromit, take the wheel," said Wallace, literally handing Gromit the steering wheel. Gromit had to slide over and put the steering wheel back on, while Wallace heroically climbed out of the van window and jumped across towards the bike. He landed sitting down on the front mudguard of the bike, facing the panicking lady.

"Don't fret, madam!" he shouted. Wallace turned towards the van and yelled to Gromit: "Teacakes, lad! The wholemeal fruit! On my knees!"

With precise aim, Gromit threw the tea-cakes and Wallace caught them between his knees, squeezing them on to the front wheel like brake pads. Wallace had calculated that the strength of his thigh muscles combined with texture and consistency of the teacakes should cause enough friction to slow the bike down. And it worked at first, but soon the buns began to smoke.

"Ohhh . . ." panicked Wallace. "We should have tried the granary rolls!" He turned to see where they were heading – straight for the Town Zoo!

"Oh 'eck!" he cried, desperately trying to

think of another plan, but the bike was gaining even more speed now, with Wallace's weight on the front. Things weren't looking good . . .

Chapter 3

Crocs Away!

The bike whizzed through the zoo gates, with Wallace, the Bake-O-Lite girl and the poodle all clutching on tightly. Its front wheel smashed into the wall of the crocodile pit and all three of them were propelled over the handlebars towards the waiting reptiles.

Wallace managed to stop himself from falling by catching his feet on the edge of the wall. He grabbed the ankle of the Bake-O-Lite girl just in time, and held on as tightly as he could. Only Wallace's toes were stopping them both from following the poodle down into the pit. And she was falling towards the open jaws of a hungry crocodile.

It was Gromit who saved her. Armed only with a French stick, he heroically dived down, grabbing the Bake-O-Lite girl's hat as he passed, just as Tarzan would grab a vine. Gromit knew that, at some point, the elastic on the hat would snap back. He wedged the French stick into the crocodile's mouth and grabbed the poodle just as the elastic reached full stretch. As it retracted, Gromit and the poodle were pulled from the crocodile's mouth and then catapulted out of the pit to safety.

Wallace helped the Bake-O-Lite girl back over the wall.

"Are you all right, Miss?" he fussed.

"I do apologise," she purred. She fluttered her eyelashes at Wallace, and despite her increased age and waistline, he was instantly besotted.

"It's an honour to be of help," he said.

"I must get those brakes seen to," she giggled. "We're so grateful, aren't we Fluffles?" They both looked down at the little poodle, who was safely back by her mistress's side. She was shaking, which Wallace thought was quite understandable after all she'd been through. Poor little pooch.

"Fluffles!" repeated the lady, but it was more like a command this time. The dog jumped up and trotted over to Wallace. Unexpectedly, she leapt into his arms and began to lick his face.

"Oh, it was nothing," laughed Wallace. "What a lovely little doggy!" Every bit as charming as her owner, Wallace thought.

Gromit looked over at the poodle in Wallace's arms. Was it just canine jealousy, or was there something strange about this dog's behaviour? He picked up the bicycle to check the brakes but to his surprise they seemed to be working perfectly now. Now that was odd, Gromit thought. Very odd indeed.

The lady introduced herself to Wallace. "My name's Piella. Piella Bakewell," she said.

"Oh," said Wallace. "I know who you are, Miss." He launched into the Bake-O-Lite jingle: *"Light as a feather . . . you're the Bake-O-Lite girl!"*

"That's me!" said Piella brightly.

"I'm Wallace," he said eagerly. "I'm in bread myself."

He didn't mention that the mill was like a shrine to the Bake-O-Lite girl. The bakery clock was in the shape of the Bake-O-Lite balloon and its pendulum was Piella on her swing. They had a Bake-O-Lite teapot, too, and even Wallace's bedding looked like a Bake-O-Lite advert. Piella's face was everywhere.

"Are you still ballooning, Miss?" Wallace asked innocently.

Piella thought he was referring to her inflated size. "I do beg your pardon?" she said, offended but trying to hide it.

"Oh, no, no . . ." Wallace stammered, trying to recover the situation. He felt the blood rush to his cheeks. He'd meant no offence. Quite the opposite. He just wanted to keep Piella talking so he could gaze at her loveliness for a little bit longer. "I mean the Bake-O-Lite balloon," he said. "Do you still fly it?"

"Oh, I see," said Piella, looking wistful.

Whenever anyone reminded her of that hot-air balloon, it took her back in time. It had been a magical feeling, floating silently through the sky, airy and weightless. "No, not any more," she said flatly.

They looked into one another's eyes until Wallace looked away awkwardly. The conversation was taking a turn for the worse, when it had started out so well.

"Well, better be going," he said, hoping the embarrassing redness had faded from his cheeks. "Back to the grind, as it were. Goodbye, Miss Bakewell."

"Oh, Mr Wallace," she protested, her charm suddenly returning. "I'd rather say 'Au revoir'!"

Wallace brightened. He didn't understand French, but he thought this meant something about seeing one another again.

"Oui, oui!" Wallace responded. He didn't want to seem uncultured, but that was the only French he knew. "And bon appetit, Madame!"

Chapter 4

Until We Meet Again

In the bakery the next day, Gromit was working hard as usual, while Wallace was creating a little sculpture of Piella from a cottage loaf. He was singing the Bake-O-Lite jingle and sighing a great deal.

"Fancy that, Gromit," he said for the fifth time. "It's not every day you meet the girl of your dreams, is it lad?"

Gromit rolled his eyes. Wallace was acting

like a lovesick puppy and he wanted him to snap out of it. There was work to be done.

At that moment, the doorbell rang. Wallace was taken aback when he opened the door to find Piella and Fluffles standing there.

"We were just passing by, going for a walk, and Fluffles insisted on dropping in, hoping you would join us," Piella explained. "Please say yes. She'd be so disappointed, wouldn't you Fluffles?"

Fluffles looked up at Wallace. She didn't look as if she'd be disappointed.

"Wouldn't you Fluffy!" Piella repeated, giving Fluffles a little nudge with her foot.

Fluffles jumped up with a start. She began to pull on Wallace's trouser leg.

Goodness, thought Wallace, *maybe she would be disappointed!* He was touched, but then he always knew he had a way with dogs.

"Oh well," said Wallace. "If you insist. But I'm in me work things."

Piella chuckled. "I like a man in uniform!"

The combined charms of Piella and Fluffles had worked perfectly on Wallace. "Manage without me, won't you lad?" he shouted to Gromit, then disappeared out of the door. Gromit was left alone again, with a list of jobs to do and no one to help him.

And that's how things continued. Every day Piella turned up with another plan for the day – feeding the ducks, going to the funfair, punting along the canal, tango lessons . . . Wallace was enjoying the attention and the female company. He couldn't believe the Bake-O-Lite girl, the girl of his dreams, was suddenly in his life and interested in him! Every morning he left the house without a thought for his faithful pal Gromit, who was left to run the bakery single-handedly. When Wallace and Piella returned home after their fun-filled days, they dumped their coats on Gromit and expected him to make the tea. But the real test of Gromit's patience came in the evenings when they kept him awake with their laughter and chatter. Even pulling a pillow over his head didn't help. Nevertheless, Gromit still got up at the crack of dawn to bake and deliver the bread to the Top Bun customers.

He could never have anticipated what was about to happen next.

Chapter 5

A Woman's Touch

Gromit was returning from his delivery round one morning when he noticed the dustbin was overflowing with stuff. On inspection, he realised that it was all *his* stuff – his precious collection of records, his much-loved books, his Beagle Comics and his favourite toys. Puzzled and cross, Gromit walked into the house. The first thing he saw was a photo of Wallace, Piella and Fluffles hanging on the wall. Then he heard

Wallace's voice behind the door.

"Oh, it makes a change, doesn't it my fudge cake?" said Wallace. "Gromit's going to love this."

Wallace couldn't have been more mistaken.

When Gromit pushed open the door, he looked around, stunned by what he saw. He barely recognised the place. There were vases of flowers everywhere, and the room was spotlessly clean. Not a crumb on the floor or a dog's hair on the cushions. Wallace was tucking into a big plate of bangers and mash. He looked up and smiled at Gromit, who returned the look, but his expression was far from happy. First he looked confused, then hurt, and finally very cross indeed. What on earth was going on?

"I thought you could do with a woman's touch around the house," said Piella. "You naughty slovenly boys!"

"What d'you think, Gromit?" asked Wallace with a mouthful of mash. "Wouldn't know it was our place, would you lad?"

Gromit glared at him for a moment and then turned round and retreated upstairs to his bedroom. But even there, he couldn't find sanctuary. Opening his bedroom door was just as much of a shock as opening the door downstairs. He had forgotten about the dustbin full of his stuff, but now he saw that Piella had been tidying his room, too. Everything was neatly arranged, and anything that didn't have a place had been thrown away. There were pretty cushions on the bed and a vase full of flowers on his bedside table. Furious, Gromit grabbed the flowers and threw them in the bin. How dare she . . . !

There was a knock on his door.

Gromit stopped in his tracks and then quickly grabbed the flowers out of the bin and popped them back into the vase. He didn't want Piella to see what he really thought of her bedroom makeover. However, to his surprise, when he opened the door, it wasn't Piella standing there. It was Fluffles. She was carrying a box containing stuff she had rescued from the dustbin. She held it out to him, as if it were a peace offering.

Gromit eyed her suspiciously, but then something about her made him relax. Maybe it was because she was a dog? Maybe it was because she was a *pretty* dog? But more likely it was because she seemed to understand . . . which was more than Wallace did!

Gromit took the box gratefully and their paws touched for an instant. It was like an electric shock for both of them. Fluffles drew back and Gromit looked away bashfully. His eyes fell on his *Puppy Love* record in the box. How embarrassing to own something so soppy! He blushed and shrugged. Fluffles chuckled. She thought it was sweet that Gromit liked romantic music. All the other dogs she'd met were just into street sounds and howling.

"Fluffles!" came Piella's call from downstairs. "Where are you? Time we were off!"

Alarm flashed across Fluffles' face and she rushed off without looking back.

Chapter 6

Gromit Discovers a Terrible Secret

"Love is a many splendoured thing, Gromit," said Wallace yawning. "But it doesn't half tire you out!" He was about to go up to bed when he noticed Piella's purse on the stairs. "Oh 'eck," he said. "I must return it forthwith."

Wallace opened the front door to discover it was tipping down with rain.

He hesitated. On second thoughts, maybe it was a bit late and he *was* very tired.

"Gromit . . . ?" he called.

So it was Gromit who headed out into the rain, which got heavier and heavier as he drove towards Piella's house. When he got out of the van, it had turned into a nasty thunderstorm.

Gromit looked up the large and forbidding mansion. There were no lights in the windows, and none of the warm glow that emanates from most houses at night. The building looked abandoned, and perhaps it was, thought Gromit when he found the front door slightly open. Summoning up his courage, he peered inside to see if there was any sign of life. What he saw made him feel uneasy. The hallway was grand but sparsely furnished and it looked dark and eerie. There were no flowers in vases or happy pictures on the walls. Surely this couldn't be Piella's home?

Gromit noticed a thin crack of light underneath

one of the doors leading off from the hall. He was about to go in, when he looked again at the dark corners of the hallway, wondering if something or someone was lurking there, watching, waiting for him to enter the house. He strained his eyes, willing them to get used to the dark. Then a bolt of lightning flashed overhead and lit everything up for a second. All it revealed was just more emptiness. Gromit weighed up the choices in his mind. If this wasn't Piella's house, what was he walking into? And if it was, *why* was it so spooky and unwelcoming?

But Gromit had a job to do, so he gingerly tiptoed across the hallway towards the light and the faint sound of a TV. Just as he was about to knock on the door, another crash of thunder made Gromit leap out of his skin. The lightning flash had lit up a room upstairs and cast shadows on the walls. They were not normal shadows. It looked as if the room was full of people, but there was no noise and no movement. In fact, it looked as if the room was full of bakers in their baker's hats! There was another lightning flash and yet again baker-shaped shadows were cast on the walls. Fearful but puzzled, Gromit had to investigate. Something was not right – *really* not right. He crept up the stairs towards the room . . .

Gromit's eyes widened when he peered in through the door. The chamber was full of wooden tailor's dummies arranged around a large bed. Each dummy was wearing a baker's hat and apron and had a number stuck to its face. Gromit glanced from one dummy to another. The numbers went up to twelve, but there was a thirteenth dummy in the corner with no apron, no hat and no number. With the storm raging outside, the shadows and the wind made the dummies seem ghostly – almost like the living dead.

Gromit's eyes fell on a big red album on the dressing table. Putting down Piella's purse, he opened the cover slowly. On the first page, underneath a big number '1', there was a picture of Piella with a man in a baker's hat. The label underneath read 'Pat O'Cake' and someone had drawn a big red cross over the man's face.

Gromit's mind was racing. So this was Piella's house, but what did everything mean?

He turned round to look at tailor's dummy number one. He looked back at the album and turned the page to see baker number two with Piella. His name was Ken Wood (a chef), and he too had a red cross drawn over his face. Page after page showed pictures of Piella with bakers –

Crusty Rolls . . . Peter Bread . . . Shorty Shortcake . . . Wayne Scales . . . all crossed out. But it was when Gromit got to baker number twelve that his suspicions were confirmed. Gromit recognised this baker from the front page of *The Daily Grind.* It was Baker Bob, who had been battered to death with his own rolling pin!

Shaking, Gromit turned the page to number thirteen. Staring out at him was Wallace, beaming with happiness next to Piella. The only difference was that Wallace's face had not been crossed through.

Gromit looked round at the thirteenth tailor's dummy. Then he looked back at the photograph. His nose went dry and his hackles went up. There was now no doubt in his mind. Wallace was going to be Piella's thirteenth victim! Piella was the cereal killer!

Gromit reeled back and knocked into one of the tailor's dummies. It toppled over, knocking into another. One by one, they all fell like dominoes and clattered to the floor.

The door downstairs opened. Piella had heard the noise and was starting to climb the stairs. Gromit looked round in a panic. Where could he hide?

As Piella entered her bedroom, she turned on the light. She cast her eyes over the room but everything looked fine. She was confused. She definitely heard a noise but nothing was out of place. Gromit had worked like a dog to get everything back in position. But where was he now?

"That's funny," Piella said to Fluffles who had followed her up the stairs. "I'm sure I heard something."

Then she looked over at the dressing table. The album was still open. Would that give Gromit away?

"Oh, there it is," she said, closing the album and picking up the purse that Gromit had left there. "It must have been there all along." And with that she relaxed and got ready for bed.

Meanwhile, Fluffles remained confused. Her doggy senses told her that something wasn't quite right. She looked under the bed but found nothing.

"Fluffles!" barked Piella. "Stop dithering around and go to bed! Big day tomorrow. Our final baker is nicely buttered up!"

Piella put her dressing gown away in the wardrobe. As she closed the door, if she had looked, she would have seen Gromit reflected in the mirror. He was on the ceiling, stretched out on the wheel-shaped light and clinging on with super-canine strength.

Luckily, Piella turned away from the mirror. Fluffles, however, didn't. She saw Gromit, but to his amazement she didn't give him away. She just crawled into her rather plain little bed and, when Piella turned off the light, they both went to sleep.

Unfortunately for Gromit, in his haste he had chosen the worst place in the room to hide. The light was right above Piella's bed so there was no way of getting down without waking her up. He was stuck there until morning, and even then she might notice him.

As the lightning flashed, Gromit could do nothing but watch Piella snore beneath him. It was almost as loud as the thunder outside.

He knew that if he gave in to his need for sleep he would fall right on top of Piella. He had to keep himself awake . . . somehow!

Wallace has converted his house into a windmill. Cracking sails (especially if you forget to duck)!

It's a bad time for bakers, with a cereal killer on the loose.

It's love at first sight for Wallace when the Bake-o-Lite girl crusts the horizon.

It's a dog's life for Gromit, working all hours in the bakery while Wallace moons about with Piella.

Who could resist this vision of loveliness?

It takes courage for Gromit to go to Piella's house alone.

Tea-time goes with a bang when Piella provides the cake!

At the touch of a paw, electricity sparks between Gromit and Fluffles.

Chapter 7

And it Gets Worse!

Of course it was impossible for Gromit to stay awake all night, but his claws were embedded into the wooden light above Piella's bed so he didn't fall. He woke with a jolt, unwittingly pulling his claws free so he fell. The events of the night before flashed through his mind in the second it took him to reach the bed below. In his semi-awake state he heard Piella's scream, but when he landed he discovered it was just a dream. The bedroom was now bathed in sunshine and the bed was neatly made. Piella and Fluffles had gone.

Gromit remembered Piella's final words. "Big day tomorrow," she had said. "Our final baker is nicely buttered up!" That could only mean one thing. Today was the day that the cereal killer was going to strike again, and Gromit knew that her final baker was Wallace!

Gromit grabbed Piella's album and dashed out of the room. He had to get home to raise the alarm.

The Top Bun van screeched to a halt outside the house and Gromit ran in with the album. He found Wallace in the lounge.

"Oh, hello stranger!" said Wallace, greeting him with a smile. "Where've you been?"

Gromit wasted no time. He thrust the album at Wallace.

"Woah, lad. Hold your horses," Wallace laughed. "I've got something to tell you first, old pal . . . Haven't we, dearest?"

Gromit reeled round to see Piella and Fluffles entering the room. Piella was holding out her hand to show Gromit the large ring on her finger.

"Of course, my little cheesecake," Piella responded. "Wallace and I are engaged to be married!" Then she added chillingly, "Till death do us part!"

Gromit was horrified. No! NO! This couldn't be happening! He quickly hid the album behind his back. He'd have to show it to Wallace later. But unfortunately Piella had seen it.

"I think congratulations are in order, lad?" said Wallace, oblivious to everything.

Piella saw her chance. "I can see he's *dying* to give me a great big kiss," she said, lunging at Gromit with open arms. She gave Gromit a long, lingering embrace, and as she was doing so she prised the album from his paws. Gromit tried to hang on – it was the only evidence he had – but Piella didn't release him until she had it. Then she went back to Wallace's side, slipping the album into the fire as she went. Gromit watched as his only proof went up in smoke.

Piella met Gromit's steely glare. "I know we're going to get on like a house on fire," she said, pointedly. "One big happy family."

Gromit's heart sank. He had to protect Wallace from this baker-bashing maniac.

Chapter 8

You Can't Be Too Careful

Gromit went into overdrive to protect his master from Piella. He grabbed the wheelbarrow from the garden and gathered together every single potential weapon in the house. Into the barrow went the ceremonial swords from the wall, the fire irons from the fireplace and all the sharp metal objects. He almost forgot about the rolling pin in the kitchen, but then he scooped that up too. He pushed the over-loaded wheelbarrow out into the garden and locked everything away in the shed. Then he got out his copy of *Electronic Surveillance for Dogs* and set to work. If Piella brought any weaponry into the house, she'd have to get it past him first.

And it wasn't long before she was on the doorstep again, this time carrying a basket containing a pot of steaming soup.

"Hello, my vanilla slice," she said as Wallace opened the door.

"Come on in my . . ." Wallace struggled for the appropriate words, ". . . um, sponge cake," he added awkwardly.

As Piella stepped into the hallway, flashing lights and sirens went off. She had walked through a metal detector the size of an airport bomb scanner. Gromit was looking very official, sitting at a desk with a SURVEILLANCE hat on. He jumped up and frisked Piella like a security guard and confiscated her soup ladle.

"Oh," she squealed.

"You'll have to forgive him, my petal," said Wallace. "He's been a bit security conscious of late."

Piella narrowed her eyes at Gromit. "Well, you can't be too careful these days," she said. "What with a serial killer on the loose . . ." She grabbed her basket back from Gromit and took it through to the kitchen.

"Now how about a nice spot of cock-a-leekie soup?" she asked Wallace.

"Oho, smashing!" he replied, picking up a bloomer loaf. "I've got just the bread to go with it." He went to grab a bread knife, but the knife block was empty. He opened the drawers and realised there wasn't one kitchen utensil to be found.

"That dog!" Wallace tutted, puzzled by Gromit's strange behaviour. Still, perhaps his friend was just jealous. Wallace made a mental note to spend a little more time with Gromit. He was obviously feeling left out.

Meanwhile, Gromit was still in a heightened state of alert. He threw Piella's ladle into the shed and rushed back into the house. He heard Wallace's voice in the dining room.

"Smells delicious . . ." Wallace was saying.

Then he heard Piella's voice: "I do hope you like it, my shortcrust. It's my own very special recipe . . ."

POISON! Gromit hadn't thought of that! He dashed into the dining room just as Wallace was lifting a spoonful of cock-a-leekie soup to his mouth. Gromit threw himself in between Wallace and the spoon and, in a gesture of pure self-sacrifice, he ate the soup. Then he lifted the bowl and sniffed it.

"Hey!" said Wallace angrily. This time Gromit had gone too far. Feeling left out was something Wallace could understand, but getting in between him and his food was a different matter! "What are you playing at, lad? This is getting ridiculous."

It was Piella who stepped in. "Oh, Wallace," she said soothingly. "He just wants a bit of attention, that's all."

She bent down to pat Gromit under the table.

"Now, my little poochie-woochie . . ." she cooed at Gromit. "Let Auntie Piella sort you out." Her smile became crooked and evil just before she sank her *own* teeth into her *own* arm. Piella howled and showed Wallace the bold red teeth marks in her flesh.

"He bit me!" she cried.

Wallace's face fell. "Eh?" he said in disbelief.

"I was just trying to help and he bit me, Wallace!"

Wallace looked at Piella's arm and then at Gromit. Had Gromit really done such a thing? He was shocked, and he wasn't the only one. Gromit stood frozen to the spot, gazing at Piella. This woman, he thought, was not just dangerous. She was stark raving mad.

"Gromit!" Wallace said raising his voice. "How dare you bite my betrothed! That's very impolite."

"Don't be too hard on him, Wallace," cooed Piella, still very much in control of the situation.

"Just a *little* punishment. That's all." She grinned at Gromit. If Wallace hadn't intended to punish Gromit, he would have to now.

Gromit saw that this was all part of Piella's plan. He shot a look at Fluffles, who had watched all of this with growing concern. But could she and, more importantly, would she do anything to help?

With Piella's encouragement, Wallace put a muzzle on Gromit and chained him up in the kitchen. There was a huge pile of dirty dishes for him to wash.

"Oh, I'm surprised at you Gromit. I really am," Wallace scolded. He was going to have to teach Gromit that he wasn't top dog in the house anymore.

Then Piella called from upstairs. "Oh, Wallace!" she trilled. "My sugar dumpling! Have you got a mo?"

"On my way, cupcake!" Wallace called back, and with that he hooked the padlock key by the door. "You'll not leave this kitchen until you've done every last one," he said harshly. "I don't know. Taking a bite out of my lovely fiancée. It really is the limit!"

Gromit watched Wallace disappear upstairs. His desperation grew. There was no way he was going to be able to protect Wallace now.

Chapter 9

Fluffles to the Rescue

Upstairs, Piella was ready to put the last part of her evil plan into effect. Wallace was about to become her next victim. She was standing high on a ledge above all the dangerous mill machinery when Wallace joined her upstairs.

"I'm such a silly sausage," she said, pointing to her shoe that had fallen into the master cog. "It just sort of fell off my foot."

Piella sounded innocent, but Gromit knew

she had murder in mind.

"Stay well back, my precious," said Wallace, heroically. "Leave it to me."

"Oh you're so brave, Wallace . . ." Piella cooed, but her tone changed as she winked at Gromit downstairs, ". . . my minced pie," she added. She started to advance on Wallace, who was leaning over perilously towards the master cog, trying to grab the shoe.

Gromit looked on, aghast. He tried to grab the keys to unlock himself but they were just out of reach. He looked round urgently for some help. Where was Fluffles? She had disappeared, just when he needed her. He looked up again to see Piella about to push Wallace into the gears . . . !

Suddenly a large bag of flour swung across and hit Piella smack in the face. The blow knocked her down the stairs and the bag burst all over her, covering her in white powder.

"Got it!" cried Wallace as he retrieved the shoe, unaware of what had just happened. As he pulled himself back to safety, he realised Piella had gone. He rushed down the stairs and found her flat on her back at the bottom, covered in flour.

"Are you all right, my flower?" he asked. "Oh!" he laughed. "Flour! Get it? Flour!" He went to help her up.

"Get your hands off me," she barked. "You half-baked halfwit!" She was furious that her plan had been scuppered. And even more furious that Wallace was making a joke of it. "I hate flour! I hate bread! And I HATE bakers, you utter and complete fruitcake!"

Wallace was completely taken aback by the venom in her voice. "Oh! That's a bit steep, isn't it my sweet?"

Piella pulled off her engagement ring and hurled it at him. She grabbed her shoe and yelled for Fluffles, who had suddenly reappeared downstairs.

"I want a word with you back home . . ." Piella growled. She grabbed Fluffles and carried her out, slamming the door.

Wallace was speechless.

The next day, Wallace was sitting at the dining table, staring at the engagement ring. He was heartbroken. He couldn't understand what had happened.

Gromit came in with a tray of tea, some bread and a plateful of Wallace's favourite cheeses to cheer him up.

"Oh, thanks old pal," said Wallace, forcing

a smile. "I don't understand women," he said, shaking his head and shrugging. "One minute they love bakers, the next minute they hate bakers. And I'm not a fruitcake, am I lad?"

Gromit put a sympathetic paw on his master's shoulder.

"I suppose you can't be everyone's cup of tea, can you?" Wallace said, philosophically.

Gromit raised his teacup to that. He was glad to see the back of that mad, murdering monster. He never wanted to see her EVER again.

At that point, the doorbell rang. Wallace dragged himself up and trudged to the door. When he opened it, his heart lifted. It was Piella, and she was holding a large gift-wrapped box.

"I'm so sorry, Wallace. So, so sorry . . ." her voice was soft and sweet. "I don't know what came over me. Apart from the flour of course!"

she laughed. Wallace laughed nervously with her, not quite knowing if she was going to turn again. She hadn't found that joke very funny yesterday.

"Let's forget about it," she said. "Here's a cake to celebrate." Piella marched into the house and Gromit's security scanner lit up and the sirens sounded.

"Oops!" said Piella craftily. "Must be my keys!" And she threw her handbag carelessly to Gromit.

Gromit was at first angry to see Piella, but his anger turned to concern when he realised Fluffles wasn't with her.

Wallace was still oblivious. "Celebrate?" he didn't understand what Piella was talking about.

"Us!" said Piella. "Getting back together again, you gooseberry fool!"

That lifted Wallace's spirits completely. He

had his fiancée back AND she'd brought cake!

"We could have that with our four o'clock tea," he said. "Won't you join us?"

"I would," replied Piella, "but Fluffles isn't too well. Why don't you two celebrate? Must fly!" And with that, she picked up her handbag and disappeared.

Gromit's ears had pricked up at the mention of Fluffles. Unwell? Gromit didn't believe it. Maybe Piella suspected it was Fluffles who pushed the flour bag at her yesterday, but would she be crazy enough to harm her own dog? He had to find Fluffles – and fast.

Chapter 10

Roll on Tea-Time!

Gromit arrived at Piella's mansion. This time the door was firmly shut.

Gromit started to climb up the drainpipe towards an open window in Piella's bedroom. He peered through and looked over towards Fluffles' bed. There was a shivering lump underneath the blanket. Gromit presumed it was Fluffles, shaking with fear.

He climbed through the window and made his

way towards the bed, but when he pulled back the blanket he saw that it was a trap. The lump was a clockwork monkey.

Before Gromit could react, Piella had grabbed him by the throat!

"Got you, you meddling mutt!" she snarled. "So nice of you to come. Pity you'll miss your master's tea party." She glanced out through the window towards Wallace's windmill. "But it'll still go off with a bang!"

Gromit followed her gaze towards the windmill. What did she mean, 'go off with a bang'? Gromit's eyes scanned the horizon for the church clock tower. He saw that it was four minutes to four. Four minutes to go before teatime. Four minutes to go before . . . BANG! The cake! *Piella's cake must be a bomb!*

Across town, Wallace was humming to himself while preparing the tea. He opened Piella's box and his eyes widened. Inside was a huge cake with one little candle. It looked scrumptious, and the candle was a nice touch – it would make his tea all the more special.

"Mmm!" he said, rubbing his hands together. "Get the kettle on Gromit!" He didn't realise that Gromit was half-way across town, in the grasp of his fanatical fiancée.

Piella and Gromit were both looking at the clock tower. The hands moved. It was now two minutes to four.

"Nearly time for the fireworks," Piella said chirpily. "Well, you know what they say about keeping pets indoors!" She pushed Gromit into the storeroom where she had locked Fluffles the night before. Gromit landed by Fluffles' side and they exchanged worried looks, but at least he had found her *and* she was safe.

"I'll deal with you two later," said Piella, as she slammed the door shut. They heard her laugh as she walked away.

Meanwhile, at the mill, Wallace had found a box of matches.

"Come on, lad!" he called out to Gromit. "What's keeping you?" He couldn't have known that his faithful pal had been locked in a store cupboard by his beloved.

But luckily for all of them it wasn't just any old store cupboard – it was a Bake-O-Lite treasure trove, with one very useful piece of Bake-O-Lite memorabilia.

Just as Piella was crowning the thirteenth dummy with a baker's hat in anticipation of the massive explosion that was just a minute away, she noticed something strange pass her bedroom window. Her mouth fell open. She couldn't believe it! It was the Bake-O-Lite balloon. With Fluffles and Gromit on board! They had wasted no time in searching the cupboard for something to help them escape, but who would have thought that the balloon's automatic inflation mechanism would still be working after all these years. While Fluffles had made sure the swing was still firmly fixed, Gromit had broken the window latch with a Bake-O-Lite key ring, and they were set to go within seconds.

Now they were a high-flying canine crack team, on their way to rescue Gromit's master from impending disaster.

"Curse that balloon . . ." Piella yelled out of the window. She was purple with rage as she waved her fist at them. "And curse that prevailing south-westerly!" Because even the wind was in Gromit and Fluffles' favour now. It had picked up to a near gale and was carrying them towards the Top Bun windmill at a steady rate of knots. They would be there in no time . . . but would it be soon enough?

Chapter 11

Bombs Away!

As the church clock began to strike four, Gromit jumped from the Bake-O-Lite balloon through the dining-room window like an SAS commando. Wallace was just about to strike a match.

"Oh, there you are," said Wallace, nonplussed at Gromit's dramatic entry. He lit the candle. "I think these matches are a bit –" Gromit picked up a vase of flowers and threw the water over the match, and over Wallace – "damp!" Wallace concluded, looking down at his drenched clothes and the drenched cake. But the candle relit.

"Ha, ha!" laughed Wallace. "It's one of those joke candles, lad!"

Gromit was dismayed. If he couldn't put out the fuse, he had to get rid of the bomb. He grabbed the cake and started to run.

"Oi!" shouted Wallace in alarm. "Where are you going with that cake?" He launched himself at Gromit and rugby tackled him to the ground. The cake fell from Gromit's hands and the box came apart, revealing the bomb inside. Its fuse was still alight and burning down quickly.

"Gromit!" cried Wallace, finally grasping the situation. "It's a bomb! The cake's a bomb!" Gromit rolled his eyes. Talk about stating the obvious!

"Wait a minute!" continued Wallace. "You don't think Piella could be . . ."

". . . The cereal killer?" It was Piella who finished Wallace's sentence. She stepped into the room, holding Fluffles by the throat. "Well done, Wallace. Sharp as a brick! Now do exactly as I say or Fluffles gets snuffled."

There seemed to be no stopping this woman.

But Fluffles bit back.

"Oww!" yelled Piella, as she dropped the poodle. Gromit seized the moment and grabbed the bomb. Piella raised her hand to hit Fluffles. "You've crossed me once too often, you treacherous little . . ." But she stopped when she saw Gromit disappearing with the bomb.

"Get that thing away, lad," Wallace called to Gromit. "It could do someone a mischief."

Gromit ran upstairs and went to throw the bomb out the window, but down below he could see two proud ducks with their five little ducklings. He couldn't drop a bomb down there. So he ran to the opposite window. He was about to make the throw when he saw two nuns walking along the street with kittens in their arms. That was no good either! So he ran to the next window and was about to lob the bomb out across the border into Yorkshire, but Piella got to the window first. She whacked him with a large bread shovel, knocking him down the stairs. The bomb flew out of his hands and disappeared out of the window.

"Confound it!" raged Piella. She picked up a spanner. "I'll just have to do this by hand!" And she came at Wallace with the blunt instrument.

"But Piella . . ." pleaded Wallace as he backed away. "You're the Bake-O-Lite girl!"

It was just the wrong thing to say.

"WAS the Bake-O-Lite girl!" she raged. Piella wielded the spanner at Wallace. "I ate too much, you see," she said, swiping at him so viciously that he dodged and fell. He scrambled along a duct in the floor. Piella ripped off the metal grille above him that protected him from her blows. "I couldn't ride the balloon anymore," she said, swinging the spanner once more as Wallace continued to scramble along the duct. "So they dropped me!" Wallace had reached a dead end. Piella ripped off the last metal grille above him. "A curse on bakers and their loathsome confections!" she yelled, and the spanner came down for the final, fatal blow.

Gromit stepped in and stopped it with a French stick.

"Oh! Well done, lad," said Wallace. "Must be yesterday's." And it was a blessing the bread was so stale, because it made a useful weapon for Gromit. He twirled it like a ninja.

"That's it lad," said Wallace, cheering him on. "Use your loaf!" But in his excitement, Wallace knocked a lever that activated a trap door below Gromit. The dog disappeared down into a large mixing bowl.

"Oops!" said Wallace, as Piella picked up Gromit's French stick and came towards him. "But Piella," he pleaded. "This is murder! Where will it all end?"

"With you, Wallace," she sneered. "My thirteenth . . . My baker's dozen!"

So that was it. Wallace was to be her last victim. Thirteen dead bakers – her sick and twisted revenge on those she felt were responsible for her increased size.

Piella's hand clenched tightly around the stale

French stick and she brought it down with such force that Wallace closed his eyes. This was it. He was toast. But again, something got in the way. Wallace opened one eye and saw the arms of the forklift truck had blocked the blow.

"Well done, la–" Wallace stopped when he saw who was at the wheel of the truck. It was Fluffles! "Er, lass," he amended.

Piella grabbed a couple of rolling pins and started twirling them like a cowboy twirling his guns. She was more than ready for a fight.

"Come to mummy, Fluffy-wuffy," she said. Obeying her mistress, Fluffles came at Piella in the forklift. Piella was forced backwards, but she wasn't going to give up easily. She had turned into a crazed maniac and was attacking the forklift and Fluffles with unbelievable strength. Wallace went to give Fluffles a hand. He picked up another rolling pin and entered the fray. "At-a-girl!" he shouted encouragingly to Fluffles. "Go for the knock-out!" The forklift arm came swinging round and accidentally knocked him out of the window. As he fell, his trousers snagged on the windmill sail and he was carried up into the air. At least he was heading out of danger, but what about Gromit?

Gromit was clambering out of the mixing bowl down in the kitchen when he saw Wallace go past the window, dangling from the sail.

"Don't worry about me, lad," Wallace called. "I'm fully in control!" But he was not the only thing snagged on the sails. Behind him was the bomb! It had fallen from the window and lodged in the sail fabric. When the sails reached their full height, Wallace became detached and he fell through the skylight at the top of the windmill. He was relieved when he landed on his bed, but his relief turned to dismay when a second later the bomb fell next to him.

"No!" he yelled. Surely there were only seconds to go before the horrible thing exploded! But his nightmare was about to get worse. Down below, Piella, in her mad frenzy, knocked the Get-U-Up lever and Wallace's bed tipped up. He began to fall down the chute, followed closely by the bomb. There was no getting away from it now!

When he landed, both Gromit and Piella froze and looked at him. Gromit had again joined Fluffles in the fight, and they had pushed Piella right to the edge of the loading hatch. She was teetering on the edge by her toes.

They gazed at Wallace as he stood up. "Anyone

seen the bomb?" he said, looking anxiously around him. It was puzzling because the bomb had been right behind him. Where could it have gone? You couldn't just lose a bomb!

Both Gromit and Piella knew exactly where it was. They could see the smoke coming from Wallace's trousers. Piella seized her moment. The Bake-O-Lite balloon was still outside the window where Gromit and Fluffles had left it, so she climbed in and turned up the gas. As she floated away she called: *"Bomb* voyage, Wallace! Your buns are as good as toasted!"

Wallace turned round to see what they had been staring at.

"Ooooh, Gromit!" he said, panicking and running around like a lunatic. "I've got a bomb in me pants! Help me, Gromit. Do something!"

Gromit looked at Fluffles, desperate for some

inspiration. What could they do? The bomb was fizzing away and the fuse was at its end. The bomb was about to explode!

Chapter 12

Great Minds Think Alike

Gromit and Fluffles had a brainwave! It came to them in an instant. They didn't have time to get rid of the bomb so they had to find a way to protect Wallace from its blast. And there was one thing that might work – dough! It was stodgy enough to absorb the impact. It was thick enough to form a protective cushion for Wallace. And it was in plentiful supply in the Top Bun bakery. It was the only hope.

Fluffles and Gromit grabbed the nozzle of the liquid dough dispenser, shoved it up Wallace's trouser leg and turned the knob up to FULL. The liquid dough oozed out of the hose. It was flowing fast, but was it fast enough?

"Ooh! It tickles," said Wallace as the dough started to fill his trousers. In a matter of seconds, his trousers were fully inflated.

Fluffles and Gromit could do nothing more. They took cover behind a table with saucepans on their heads.

And just in the nick of time.

BOOM!

The bomb exploded. Dough splattered everywhere. The windmill shook and the force of the blast propelled Piella's balloon away. When the smoke cleared inside the windmill, Wallace was still standing there, slightly shaken but still very much alive. The blast had ripped through his trousers and made a large hole in the side of the windmill. Wallace looked through the hole. Goodness gracious, he thought to himself. He didn't want to contemplate what would have happened if Gromit and Fluffles hadn't been so quick-thinking. Looking up at him from the street below were two nuns.

"Evening, sisters," Wallace called and waved. He was feeling rather lucky to be alive. The nuns turned red and scurried away. *Whatever was the matter with them?* he thought to himself, without realising that he was completely exposed – his bottom was on view to the world!

Then he noticed the Bake-O-Lite balloon gliding away in the distance. Piella had the gas burners on full blast but she was still losing height. She was frantically dropping sandbags from the balloon, but it wasn't making any difference. She was going down.

"I will be back to get you, Wallace," she yelled across the sky. "I will have my baker's dozen!"

"But Piella," Wallace called back with concern. She was still his fiancée after all. "The balloon won't hold you! You're too . . ."

Piella didn't let him finish his sentence. "They can't just drop me! I'm as light as a feather . . ." She started to flap her arms in desperation.

"Piella!" called Wallace as she plummeted. He saw where she was heading – towards the crocodile pit in the Town Zoo.

Her final tragic words floated across the sky. "I'm the Bake-O-Lite Giiiirrrrlll!" Then she disappeared into the pit. The crocodiles had never before been thrown such a large and tasty meal.

A few moments later, the balloon floated

up from the pit, without the swing and without Piella. It rose into the sky, and as it passed in front of the sun, Wallace thought he could make out the slender, beautiful figure of Piella just as she had been in the TV adverts.

"Farewell, my angel cake," called Wallace. He waved sadly. "You'll always be my Bake-O-Lite girl."

Chapter 13

A Cup of Tea Cures All

"Think I need a cup o' tea after all that," said Wallace. He turned to go downstairs. Gromit quickly covered Fluffles' eyes so she was spared the sight of Wallace's bare behind. "Care to join me, you two?"

Gromit gestured to Fluffles to go down the stairs before him, but she looked at him sadly and shook her head. She obviously didn't feel she deserved their kindness after all that they had been through.

Gromit saw her to the front door. He wished Fluffles didn't want to leave. She had saved them both. She'd stood up to Piella, that butcher of bakers, and stopped her reign of terror. To him, Fluffles was a hero.

Gromit stood at the front door, willing her to stay, but Fluffles walked down the path without looking back. It was too painful to watch her, so Gromit closed the door slowly. His heart was quietly breaking.

Wallace brought in the tea. "Never mind, lad. We've both been through the mill this week, haven't we? But at least yours wasn't a bread-hating, baker-murdering cereal killer, eh, like mine."

Gromit nodded. Wallace had a point.

"Tell you what lad," said Wallace, brightening

up. "Let's go and deliver some bread. That'll cheer us up. Prepare the rolls!" he said with a flourish, like a lord to his chauffeur.

Wallace made himself decent while Gromit loaded up the trusty van. The Top Bun team were back in business and ready to go. Wallace revved the engine and the garage door flew open, but Wallace slammed on the brakes again quickly. Fluffles was standing in front of them, tears in her eyes.

Gromit was delighted. He opened the door for her. Fluffles looked at Gromit and the open door. Her face lit up.

"Always room for a small one!" said Wallace as Fluffles jumped in the van. He popped a baker's hat on her head. She was now officially part of the Top Bun team. She selected a record from the drawer in the dashboard and slid it into the record player. It was *Puppy Love.* As the Top Bun van sped off down the street, Doggy Osmond began to howl.

For Gromit and Fluffles, it was the perfect song for a perfect ending.

Wallace & Gromit

Fancy a rib-tickler Gromit?

Why did the baker stop making doughnuts?

He got tired of the hole thing!

Ha ha!

Hee hee!

Why is Wallace a good baker?

Because he loafs about so much!

A MATTER OF LOAF & DEATH will be hitting your screens this Christmas!

The official joke book is jam-packed with gags galore, cracking capers and cheesy puns that'll make you *loaf* out loud!

EGMONT

Available to buy online at **www.egmont.co.uk** or at a retailer near you.

Wallace & Gromit

Get your oven mitts on this brilliant batch of cracking books!

IT'S A DOG'S LIFE with Gromit

IT TAKES TWO

If you love everything Wallace and Gromit you'll love these nifty little gift books - complete with quotes and illustrations from the series, plus exclusive extras!

Coming Soon! Out February 2009

FENG SHAUN

GRAND GRUB

Aardman © & TM Aardman Animations Ltd 2008

EGMONT

Available to buy online at **www.egmont.co.uk**
or at a retailer near you.